For my mom, who taught me to love art and cheesecake
—C. S.

For my dear daughter, Josephine
—C. D.

𝒜
atheneum ATHENEUM BOOKS FOR YOUNG READERS • An imprint of Simon & Schuster Children's Publishing Division • 1230 Avenue of the Americas, New York, New York 10020 • Text copyright © 2020 by Christina Soontornvat • Illustrations copyright © 2020 by Christine Davenier • All rights reserved, including the right of reproduction in whole or in part in any form. • ATHENEUM BOOKS FOR YOUNG READERS is a registered trademark of Simon & Schuster, Inc. Atheneum logo is a trademark of Simon & Schuster, Inc. • For information about special discounts for bulk purchases, please contact Simon & Schuster Special Sales at 1-866-506-1949 or business@simonandschuster.com. • The Simon & Schuster Speakers Bureau can bring authors to your live event. For more information or to book an event, contact the Simon & Schuster Speakers Bureau at 1-866-248-3049 or visit our website at www.simonspeakers.com. • The text for this book was set in Chapparal Pro. • The illustrations for this book were rendered in pen and ink washes. • Manufactured in China • 0320 SCP • First Edition • 10 9 8 7 6 5 4 3 2 1 • Library of Congress Cataloging-in-Publication Data • Names: Soontornvat, Christina, author. | Davenier, Christine, illustrator. • Title: Simon at the art museum / Christina Soontornvat ; illustrated by Christine Davenier. • Description: First edition. | New York City : Atheneum Books for Young Readers, [2020] | Audience: Ages 4 - 8. | Audience: Grades K-1. | Summary: At an art museum with his parents, Simon has trouble controlling his urges to slide on the floor, chase pigeons, and eat cheesecake at the cafe, until something special catches his eye. • Identifiers: LCCN 2019035654 | ISBN 9781534437524 (hardcover) | ISBN 9781534437531 (eBook) • Subjects: CYAC: Art museums—Fiction. | Museums—Fiction. | Art appreciation—Fiction. | Behavior—Fiction. | Family life—Fiction. • Classification: LCC PZ7.1.S677 Sim 2020 | DDC [E]—dc23 • LC record available at https://lccn.loc.gov/2019035654

Simon
at the
ART MUSEUM

Christina Soontornvat
Art by Christine Davenier

Atheneum Books for Young Readers
NEW YORK LONDON TORONTO SYDNEY NEW DELHI

"Hel-lo, art museum!" shouted Simon.

"Shhh," whispered Simon's mom.
"Sweetie, remember what we agreed about inside voices?"

Inside the museum, everyone whispered and shuffled slowly across the marble floors.

Simon shuffled too, wishing he could slipper-slide around in his socks.

Simon and his parents looked at the art together.

They looked at more art.

And then more.

So. Much. Art.

What IS it with this place? thought Simon,
before remembering that it was, in fact, an art museum.

"Is that a swimming pool?" asked Simon.

"It's a reflecting pool," whispered his dad.
"It's a work of art too, just like the paintings."

Simon casually suggested they could make the art
even better if they chased the pigeons along its edge.

After that, his parents decided they
wanted to hold his hands.

They passed the museum café, where people were eating cheesecake.

"Now *that's* what I'm talking about," said Simon.

"Don't you want to see the upstairs gallery first?" whispered his mom.

I want to see the bottom of an empty cheesecake dish, thought Simon, but he followed his parents to the elevators anyway.

The upstairs gallery was enormous.

Simon needed cheesecake, and he needed it five minutes ago.

"I'm just going to enjoy the art from a new angle for a little while," he said.

"All right," said his dad. "Just stay where we can keep an eye on you."

Simon couldn't see much art from where he was sitting.
But he could see the people who were seeing the art.

Some of it made people smile.

Some of it made them shake their heads sadly.

Some of it made them argue with one another.

One painting made two teenagers
blush bright pink and start giggling.

Another made a family turn their heads almost completely upside down.

Sometimes people got really close
to the art and squinted at it.

Other times they stood way far back.

Some walked right by the art without noticing it at all.

"Ma'am, that's a fire extinguisher."

Others noticed a little too much.

Some people looked at the art alone.

Others shared it with everyone they loved.

"This place is unbelievable," Simon whispered.

He felt right in the middle of everything,
but kind of separate, too.

Then Simon spotted something at the end of the gallery.
Was it art? He couldn't tell from here.
No one was looking at it.

He slipped off the bench and shuffled quickly toward it.

"Simon!" called his mom. "Don't run off without—"

"Shhh," whispered Simon. "You guys have to see this."

"Whoa," whispered his mom.

"Unbelievable," whispered his dad.

"Believe it," said Simon.

Later, when it was nearly closing time, Simon and his parents got ready to go.

"What a day," said Simon. "I think we saw everything in the whole museum."

"Actually," said his mom, "there's one thing we didn't see yet."